PACIOLI'S
CLASSIC ROMAN
ALPHABET

frater lucas. bartolomeus. depariobis.
deburgo sci septm

PACIOLI'S CLASSIC ROMAN ALPHABET

Stanley Morison

DOVER PUBLICATIONS, INC.

NEW YORK

Copyright

Copyright © 1994 by Dover Publications, Inc.

All rights reserved under Pan American and International Copyright Conventions.

Published in Canada by General Publishing Company, Ltd., 30 Lesmill Road, Don Mills, Toronto, Ontario.

Published in the United Kingdom by Constable and Company, Ltd., 3 The Lanchesters, 162–164 Fulham Palace Road, London W6 9ER.

Bibliographical Note

This Dover edition, first published in 1994, is an unabridged republication of the work first published in a limited edition of 397 copies by the Grolier Club, New York, in October, 1933, under the title *Fra Luca de Pacioli of Borgo S. Sepolcro*. Printer's ornaments and decorative initials that in the original edition appeared in red are here reproduced in black.

Library of Congress Cataloging in Publication Data

Morison, Stanley, 1889–1967.
    [Fra Luca de Pacioli of Borgo S. Sepolcro]
    Pacioli's classic Roman alphabet / Stanley Morison.
        p.   cm.
    Originally published: New York : Grolier Club, 1933.
    Includes bibliographical references (p.) and index.
    ISBN 0-486-27979-0 (pbk.)
    1. Pacioli, Luca, d. ca. 1514. De divina proportione.   2. Alphabets.
3. Lettering.   I. Title.
NK3615.P34   1994
745.6′1978 — dc20   93–38610
                                                              CIP

Manufactured in the United States of America
Dover Publications, Inc., 31 East 2nd Street, Mineola, N.Y. 11501

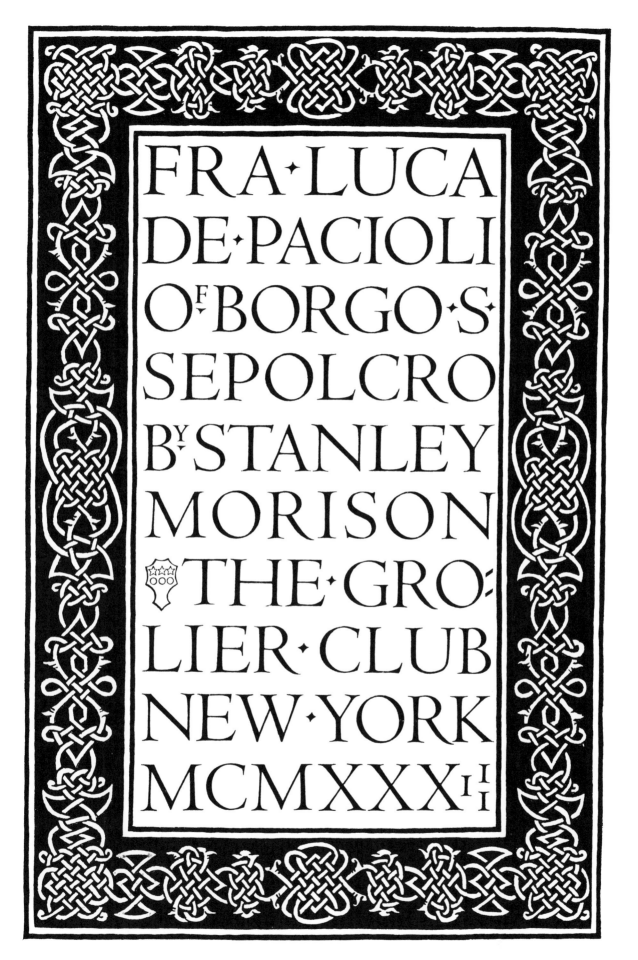

FRA·LUCA
DE·PACIOLI
OᶠBORGO·S·
SEPOLCRO
Bʸ STANLEY
MORISON
THE·GRO-
LIER·CLUB
NEW·YORK
MCMXXXII

[Original Title Page]

⤐ PREFACE ⤖

The following essay on the life of the Franciscan Friar, who earned a considerable reputation as a mathematician in the latter half of the 15th century, has here been attempted because the author left, among other literary remains, a work entitled: *De Divina Proportione*. Fra Luca is better known for his *Summa de Arithmetica* of 1494 which embodies the first printed description, in detail, of the method of book-keeping known as "Double-Entry." This treatise has been reprinted in recent years by American and English students of accountancy. The following pages describe the section of *De Divina Proportione* which comprises diagrams of the true shapes and proportions of classical Roman letters, and provides some discussion of lettering in the interests of such contemporaries of his as were architects in his native city of Borgo San Sepolcro. This discussion, although not the earliest, forms the first serious treatise of this kind to be printed and became the inspiration of the successive similar works by Albrecht Dürer and by Geofroy Tory. These latter having both been published in translation by the Grolier Club, in 1916 and 1927 respectively, it seemed to the Publications Committee of the Club that it would be only fair to the memory of Fra Luca that his prior alphabet, with his directions for making it, should be made equally available to Members. Accordingly, Pacioli's alphabet is herewith reproduced in the size of the original, and printed with a translation of the Friar's instructions. Mr Bruce Rogers, designer of the editions of the alphabets of Dürer and of Tory, is responsible for the typistry (as he perversely calls it) of the present volume also. In this connexion I should like to offer my thanks to the Committee of the Grolier Club for their readiness to authorise the printing of the book in England at the University Press, Cambridge.

It has thus been possible for me to correct the proofs in the most convenient circumstances.

The majesty of the engraved letters illustrating the Friar's work amply justifies full-size reproduction. They form a magnificent gallery of exhibits such as none can fail to admire. My own part has been limited to the compilation, from various printed sources, of the text which accompanies these reproductions. Beside Pacioli's own works I have been principally dependent upon Manzoni's *Studii di Bibliografía Analítica* (Bologna, 1882); Staigmüller's article on Pacioli in the *Zeitschrift für Mathematik u. Physik* (Hist. Abt. XXXIV, Leipzig, 1889); Cantor-Moritz' *Vorlesungen über Geschichte der Mathematik* (Leipzig, 1900); C. Winterburg's *Fra Luca Pacioli Divina Proportione* in Eitelberger-Ilg's Quellenschriften für Kunstgeschichte (Wien, 1896) and David E. Smith's *History of Mathematics* (New York, 1923). I have also consulted smaller monographs on related subjects by E. L. Jäger, P. Crivelli, V. Vianello and R. Schöne.

The "Divine Proportion," the subject matter proper of Pacioli's work from which the alphabet is taken, now known as the "Golden Section," is discussed historically in Professor R. C. Archibald's *Notes on the Logarithmic Spiral and Golden Section* (Yale, 1920) which contains a valuable bibliography.

I am obliged to Dr H. Mardersteig, of Verona, for kindly obtaining for me a photograph of the Friar's will in his holograph, preserved in the Archivio di Stato at Venice, from which is reproduced the signature below the portrait shown as the frontispiece of this book. Messrs Holme & Co., of Naples, and the authorities of the Galleria Reale kindly arranged for the portrait of Pacioli to be taken out of its frame to be photographed. Dr David Eugene Smith, of Columbia University, has generously assisted me in several conversations besides writing a note (embodied in my text) on Pacioli's importance as a mathematician. I am indebted to Mr Alan

MacDougall for help in reading Pacioli's vernacular text. Mr
Philip Hofer permitted me to borrow, for some months, his
very fine copy of *De Divina Proportione*, and allowed it to be
used for the reproduction of the letters. Mr Hofer has also
laid the book under an obligation by compiling for me the list
of the Friar's works which, having a biographical as well as a
bibliographical value, I have printed as an appendix.

Cambridge
September 1933

❧ CONTENTS ❧

PACIOLI'S
CLASSIC ROMAN
ALPHABET

Fra Luca de Pacioli

OF THE SERAPHIC ORDER OF SAINT FRANCIS

I

UCA, ZUNIPERO and AMBROGIO were the religious names of the sons of Bartolomeo, surnamed Pacioli, or Pacciuoli (apparently the correct, or at least the earliest form of the name), or in Latin Paciolus, of Borgo San Sepolcro. This small, but not undistinguished, town lay within that part of Umbria which earliest came under the influence of St Francis and of his first companions. The Seraphic saint, having preached, was well received by the inhabitants; they gave him the ancient hermitage of Mont Casale nearby, and it was during a sojourn here that there took place the incident in which St Francis commanded Brother Angelo, a noble young follower, who had repelled three famous but out-of-luck brigands, to go after them and, kneeling, to offer them bread and wine. Brother Angelo found the three not far from the Borgo, as recounted in the *Fioretti* (chapter xxvi) by Brother Leo, who also tells of the subsequent conversion of the three. Brother Angelo became Guardian of the Convent of San Casale. Again, the first place to which the saint came, still in an ecstacy, after receiving the stigmata on Mount Alvernia, was the Borgo. Unconsciously and amid cries of "Ecco il Santo" he reached a leper house a mile beyond, and later came back to Mont Casale. All this was in 1224: Francis died in 1226. But the effect on Borgo San Sepolcro remained, and the fame of St Francis was carried through the world by eyewitnesses and followers of his rule of life. Among the early Franciscan settlements Borgo San Sepolcro long remained faithful to the memory of the saint's works therein.

When the sons of Bartolomeo de Pacioli joined them, the brethren of St Francis formed the most numerous of all the Religious Orders. They had developed a school of theology; they had spread widely; Franciscan scholars were esteemed in every centre of learning, and although they were not, as such, partisans of the Renaissance, they cultivated learning. And in spite of internal dissensions, right and left wing deviations, they remained a society of poor men. For several reasons, therefore, when Luca de Pacioli found he had a vocation to the religious life, he turned to the Order of St Francis; and with the greater confidence since, with the passing of time, postulants of his particularly studious turn of mind had gained a place in its ranks.

Luca's two brothers, who also joined the Order, possessed no talent that was remarked by their contemporaries; indeed we only know of their existence from stray mention. Even the records of Luca himself are so scanty as to make his career nothing but a recital of dates, and a tale of conjectures. First, the absence of documents makes it difficult to assign, with confidence, any year as the date of the birth of Luca de Pacioli. Libri, the historian of the mathematical sciences, confidently places it in 1450, yet, as Giacomo Manzoni points out, 1440 is a safer year. At any rate, it is more likely that, since we know he was teaching mathematics at Perugia in 1475, Luca was then 35 and not 25 years of age. Secondly, all we know of the parents of Luca is that they were probably of good standing. In the preface to *De Divina Proportione*, the author takes a couple of pages to tell those to whom he addressed the book that they were citizens of no mean city; and among the prominent knights, soldiers and signiors named, he tells of the deaths of Benedetto Baiardo, "my near

kinsman," a most valiant Captain-General of infantry, and
con suo e mio nepote, "his and my nephew, Francesco Paciolo."

No date can be assigned for Luca's entry into the Franciscan Order. We know that he spent some of his early years
in Venice at the house of a merchant, Antonio de Rompiasi;
likely enough he began to interest himself in accounting while
with his Venetian friends. We know too that he attended
lectures on mathematics at this time and that he tutored his
host's three sons in the art. He was presumably ordained
priest sometime when he was about 25 years of age. The
Friar's lectures at Perugia in the year 1475 were privately
given, but in 1477 he was appointed professor of mathematics
in the University, retaining the position until 1480 and compiling during the period his first known work, namely, a
treatise on algebra, which was never printed, but remains in
manuscript in the Vatican (Codex 3129). His activities during
the 1480's seem to have been varied. He passed some time
at Zara, in what is now Jugo-Slavia, where he wrote another
Algebra, but from the end of 1485 to the spring of 1489 he
served a second period at the University of Perugia teaching
his old subject. Later in the year 1489 he lectured in Rome,
being then of sufficient distinction to lodge with the great
Leonbaptista degli Alberti. Within the next year or two,
Pacioli was called to be professor in the University of Naples.
He was now not merely a distinguished, but a famous scholar.
Powerful personages gave him their patronage. Chief among
his supporters was the famous Federigo, Duke of Urbino,
whose portrait is included in the picture of Fra Luca as a
lecturer, which remains in the Art Gallery at Naples, having
been painted during the period of his professorship in the
University. From time to time he stepped aside from his
professional to purely religious duties. The Friar was always
on good terms with his superiors and in one of his prefaces
paid a tribute to his General, Father Francesco Sanaone of

Brescia. Fra Luca preached the Lent sermons at his native
place in the year 1493, and apparently spent the rest of that
year on business for his Order at Padua, Assisi and Urbino.
In 1494 he obtained leave to go to Venice to superintend the
printing of his masterpiece, *Summa de Arithmetica, Geometria,
Proportioni et Proportionalita*, published by Paganino de Paganini
in the same year. The work brought him great reputation,
and, on the strength of it, he was for three years (1496–9)
supported as professor in the University of Milan under a
salary provided by Lodovico Sforza. Although the *Summa* was
characterised by a certain diligence it was not, for all its length,
distinguished by originality. Nevertheless, that it has some
value is attested by several modern reprints of that portion
dealing with double entry book-keeping. It is not claimed
that the Friar invented the system but it is not doubted that
he was the first writer to describe and to teach it, and modern
accountants credit the Friar's *Summa* with laying the founda-
tions of their profession. But it is not admitted by modern
mathematicians that Pacioli's writings are important. Dr
David Eugene Smith, Emeritus Professor of the History of
Mathematics in Columbia University, to whom I referred
the question of the value of Pacioli's contributions, kindly
allows me to quote his authoritative opinion.

Dr Smith writes that "Pacioli was not a mathematician
of any genius. He was merely a compiler of the ideas of
others. He had no definite opinions as to the best methods of
procedure in any branch of arithmetic, algebra, or geometry.
Even in such a simple operation as multiplication he gives
no less than eight plans, generally with the fanciful names
of the period, (1) 'Multiplicatio bericocoli vel scachierij', by
others called 'per organetto', or 'a scaletta'; (2) 'castellucio';
(3) 'ꝑ colōna ouer atauoletta'; (4) 'crocetta siue casella'; (5) 'ꝑ
q̄drilatero'; (6) 'ꝑ gelosia ouer graticola'; (7) 'repieghi'; and
(8) 'aschapeçço' (a scapezzo). None of these was original with

him, and none was given the precedence over the others. Similarly in the case of division, he gives ten methods, each with a fanciful name.

"In his treatment of algebra he showed no more originality than in his work in computation. Having no modern symbolism to assist him, his pages on the subject were confined in general to simple problems. For example, the equation which we would write as $x + x^2 = 12$ appears in the *Summa* as 'Trouame .1. n°. che giōta al suo q̄drat° facia .12.'

"His edition of Euclid (1509), interesting as an illustration of the typography of the time, made no advance in geometry and exerted little influence. His most important work, from the standpoint of mathematics, was *De Divina Proportione*, but even here there was no evidence of originality. As stated above, Pacioli was essentially a compiler, and even so he lacked in critical ability and in accuracy of statement. So serious were his defects that Jerome Cardan devoted a chapter of his *Arithmetica* (Milan, 1539) to this feature under the title 'De erroribus F. Luca equos vel transferendo non diligenter examinavit, vel describendo per incuriam praeteriit, vel inveniendo deceptus est,' and the same subject has attracted the attention of other critical writers."

It was in the year 1497 (December 14) that Luca de Pacioli completed his treatise *De Divina Proportione* and presented the manuscript to his patron. To this laborious but (*pace* Dr Smith) unoriginal work his treatise on the right proportions of roman lettering, with which this publication of the Grolier Club is concerned, was added when the book was printed, namely in 1509, by Paganino de Paganini of Venice.

The date of the Friar's death is not recorded.

{ 2 }

F the three copies of the manuscript of the treatise *De Divina Proportione* written under the author's eye, two remain. The copy made for Giangaleazzo di San Severino is to-day in the Ambrosian Library at Milan; the first copy dedicated to Lodovico Sforza is in the University Library at Geneva; but the copy made for Pietro Soderini has not been recovered. The two remaining copies both exhibit important differences from the printed text. The work as presented to Lodovico consisted of the single treatise only, *De Divina Proportione*, i.e. seventy-one chapters, concluding with a colophon and an appendix of diagrams numbering fifty-four examples of solids. This, then, is the work as completed in 1497 and presented to Lodovico Sforza. When printed by Paganini in 1509 it contained supplements; these are printed immediately after the colophon relating to the original seventy-one chapters of *De Divina Proportione*. The colophon in the Geneva manuscript of 1497 reads:

FINIS

Adi xiiii° Dicembre in Milano nel n̄r̄o almo cō-uento gouernãdo tutta la prouītia El R̄^{do} p. de sacra theol^a pfeſſore. M̄ Franco Mozanica digniſſīo miniſtro de ōlla. Mcccclxxxxviii. Sedente ſummo pontifice. Alex°. VI° Del ſuo pontificato anno VII°.

This colophon was slightly abbreviated when printed in Paganini's edition of the same text; it omits reference to the

Father-Minister who governed the Franciscan province of Milan and, using a different calendar, prints 1497 instead of 1498:

Finis a di 14. decembre in Milano nel nostro almo conuento. Mccccxcvii. Sedente summo pontifice Alexandro VI del suo pontificato anno vii.

Paganini proceeds with a dedicatory letter addressed by Pacioli to several particular pupils belonging to his native town, namely: "To his most beloved disciples and pupils Cesare del Saxo, Cera del Cera, Rainer Francesco del Pippo, Bernardino and Marsilio da Monte and Hieronymo del Secciarino, and their companions of Borgo San Sepolcro, worthy stone-cutters and zealous followers of the craft of sculpture and architecture, Fra Luca Paciuolo their fellow-countryman of the Order of Friars Minor, Professor of Theology. *Si Placet Deo.*" The Friar proceeds to say, in a familiar tone, that seeing how these friends had often asked him that, "besides the practice of arithmetic and geometry which I have given you, I would also at the same time give you some rules and methods to enable you to obtain the success in architecture that you desire, I (greatly occupied as I am by the common utility of present and future things in the preparation of mathematical works and disciplines, the printing whereof I am pushing forward with all solicitude) cannot but, if not completely, then partly at least, satisfy your very natural request; especially with regard to what it is necessary for your purpose to learn." Putting aside other undertakings, the Friar writes that he has applied himself as quickly as possible to answering their questions, and promises to give them a fuller and more complete treatise in a short time. This preface, written for his friends in the Borgo, contains a reference to *miei carnali fratelli del medesimo ordine seraphico*, i.e. his brothers in the flesh and in the Order, the Padre Zunipero and the Frate Ambrogio.

The treatise divides architecture into three chief parts, public buildings, military buildings and private dwellings. In the matter of military buildings and machines, Luca admits to some particularly keen interest, excusing himself for that "all the world knows our Borghesi are ready for everything both on foot and on horseback." Meditating on the valour of his towns-folk reminds the good Friar of a fine battle fought before San Galeotta, in which one Antonello, after campaigning on behalf of Venice by the side of Federigo of Urbino against the Romagnans, retired with fever to Urbino where he died fortified by the presence of Luca's two brothers in the Order of St Francis.

Excited, one supposes, by this memory, the Friar is led on to boast to the peaceful followers of the art of stone-cutting at Borgo San Sepolcro, that it was his kinsman, Baiardo, whose training methods were largely responsible for the valour of the Borghesi; and to prove this claim he proceeds to invoke his readers' admiration towards one or two knights whom Baiardo taught to fight. There was Gnagni della Pietra who, with his bill, cast to earth at one blow the head of Tari-paver, and "of whom there is not sufficient paper to tell how bravely he always bore himself."

The exploits of other worthy mercenaries narrowly escape narration before Luca brings himself to settle down to his proper business of discussing in this second part or supplement the true proportions of walls, counterwalls, battlements, copings, towers, ravelins, bastions, casemates and the like; and, thereafter, in the third part, of rooms, antechambers, halls, porticoes, studies, kitchens, stables, theatres, baths, latrines, wells, fountains, ovens, stairs, windows, balustrades, paths, streets, markets. All these he touches on for he had, he says, and we may well believe him, argued about every one of these constructions with his many friends, living and dead, in military service.

The complete appendix itself, as added to the seventy-one chapters presented in manuscript to Il Moro in 1497, consists of twenty chapters; all more or less directly argued from "human proportions as regards the body and the limbs, for from the human body are all measures and their names derived, and in it all kinds of proportions are found from the finger of the Most High by means of the hidden secrets of nature." Forthwith from this point of view he proceeds to discuss columns and pillars, the relation of the base and of the capital to the length of a column. In the sixth chapter, which discusses cornices and entablatures, Luca writes that "It is the custom of many upon such pillars to place letters arranged in various ways which tell and declare the purpose of (the building) in the beautiful style of the ancients, in all due proportion; and the same on other summits of pillars, tablets and monuments which, beyond question, make the work very beautiful. And so to this end I have placed at the end of our book entitled *De Divina Proportione* the manner and form and all the proportions of a fine ancient alphabet by the means of which ye can write on your works whatever ye have a mind, and will undoubtedly be commended by all for so doing. Notifying you that for this reason alone have I decided to arrange it in the said form, that scribes and miniaturists who are so sparing of using it may be clear that without their pen and pencil the two mathematical lines (the curved line and the straight line) will lead them to perfection, whether they will or not, as they also do other things, inasmuch as without these it is not possible to form anything well."

Luca proceeds to instruct his readers that it was "the most excellent painter in perspective, architect, musician, and man *de tutte virtu doctato*, Leonardo da Vinci, who deduced and elaborated a series of diagrams of regular solids at the time of his sojourn in Milan." "We found ourselves there," writes the Friar, "in the years 1496 to 1499." Luca's pride in his friendship with Leonardo and his desire to give him all due credit is again proved in chapter x, "on pyramids," which concludes with a reminder that "their order and figure ye have above in this book, together with all the other bodies, from the hand of our aforesaid compatriot Leonardo da Vinci of Florence, whose designs and figures there was truly no man who could ever surpass." Luca's phrase *per masco del prelibato nostro compatriota Leonardo*, etc., cannot mean what some have taken to be the Friar's intention, i.e. that the actual drawings in the manuscript, or as others have contended, the woodcuts in the printed book, came from the hand of the artist. Luca himself says, "the most beautiful forms of the said material bodies I have with my own hands here in Milan arranged, coloured and decorated, and formed to the number of sixty among regulars and their dependents. I arranged a set of as many others for my patron San Galeazzo Sanseverino in that place, and as many more again in Florence after the example of my perpetual gonfaloniere Petro Soderino, which are at present found in his palace." Evidently the Friar means that he worked out Leonardo's ideas. Indeed the Naples portrait of Pacioli shows him lecturing with such solids. Luca's dependence upon Leonardo is a subject to which we shall need to recur later, but it is sufficient at this point to note that Luca was more inclined to boast of, than to disguise, his indebtedness to Leonardo; and, by consequence, if he had learned the shapes of the antique letters, or the method of forming them, from the same source, the Friar would have told us. Unfortunately he tells us very little about it, and his chapter xi, "Of the origins of the letters of all nations," is so corruptly printed that it is difficult to imagine that he could have examined, or approved, the book. Following his short chapter on pyramids, the Friar immediately says, somewhat conversationally, "As I remember having

said above, I have placed the ancient alphabet at the beginning
of this book to show everyone that no other than the straight
and curved lines are required," and hurries on to say that any
alphabet of whatever nation may be similarly made. Con-
fessing his own ignorance—the Friar says he could be sold by
Hebrews or Chaldeans in the market-place and the proceeds
spent on drink without his knowing it, as happened to a Moor
on the Piazza di San Marco "here in Venice" in the presence
of some fifty *degni gentilomini*—he announces his confidence in
one thing: that Greek does not change the geometrical figures,
that no language causes a square to have five angles. So much
do those know who have only taken the first step in Euclid.

By a textual dislocation (the text is not paragraphed), the
author then immediately proceeds to say of himself: "And
I have remained the Friar, as in this famous city everyone
always calls me, and I am occupied in printing my books, to
which end I am here with the licence and support of the most
Reverend Cardinal of Saint Peter-in-Chains, Vice-Chancellor
of Holy Mother Church, and nephew of our holy Lord Pope
Julius II." He does not, however, continue with any further
discourse of himself, or of Euclid, but forthwith, and without warning, returns to the subject of the first lines of this
chapter: "I tell you (*Dico a voi*) the said alphabet is very pro-
fitable for works in sculpture, on which many are wont to
use it; or for epitaphs or other writings according as you are
commanded. And assuredly they give the greatest beauty to
every work, as is evident from the triumphal arches and other
famous edifices in Rome and elsewhere." As a speculation,
the Friar ventures that letters were invented by chance—he is
thinking of alphabetical writing as such—as appears in certain
old buildings. He proves his point by saying that the porphyry
tomb opposite the Rotunda guarded by the two lions carries
cyphers and signs of pens, knives, animals, shoe-soles, birds
and pots, all used as letters. By way of concluding the whole

matter the Friar announces that at last men "fixed upon those which at present they use." Moreover, *li hano trouato el debito modo con lo circino in curua e libella recta debitamente saperle fare,* "they found out the proper way to make them with compasses for the curves and the ruler for the straight lines." He does not here go into any detail, but returns, at what the geometricians might well call a tangent, in the following chapters (xii–xviii) to talk of columns, their bases, architraves, cornices and the like.

In spite of such digression the Friar once again considers (in chapter xix) the question of alphabetical lettering according to the geometrical method of the ancients. For, now says the Friar, "You have also here, as I have told you, *l'alphabeto dignissimo antico,* the most excellent ancient alphabet, according to which you may adorn your works and inscribe what your patrons may desire, be they tombs or other works; and these assuredly even more than is needful give great beauty to the work, as is plainly to be seen in many places in Rome. Formerly it was the custom to use various metals and to affix them to their places, as is manifest by the traces in the Capitol and in the Palace of Nero. And let not scribes and illuminators complain if such necessity has brought to light the fact that the two essential lines, straight and curved, always suffice for all things which have to be made in their art, for which reason have I made the square and circle before their eyes without their pen and pencil. Again, I do this that they may see quite clearly that everything comes from the discipline of mathematics; without mentioning that their [calligraphical] forms are arbitrary."

At this point the Friar disappoints. He turns aside from the opportunity to carry further his criticism of the practice of contemporary scribes to bring his book to an end with an admonition to his friends in Borgo San Sepolcro to "confer among yourselves, one with another like good brothers, for the greater elucidation of everything, since it is easy to add to the things you have found out, as I am sure your experienced minds will do, for their own honour and that of our country, wherefrom there have always, as you will have learnt from your ancestors, issued worthy men in every art. Although the place [Borgo San Sepolcro] is small, yet it is populous, and thus gave minds of good genius, both in military matters—as we have set out briefly above—and also in other arts and sciences." "In the case of mathematicians," says Luca de Pacioli, "the repute of the Borgo is made clear by that sovereign contemporary master of painting and architecture, Maestro Pietro degli Franceschi, who, as is apparent in Urbino, Bologna, Ferrara, Rimini, Ancona, and in our own countryside, could work in oil and aquarello on wall and on canvas; especially to be noted is his work in the great chapel of the tribune of the high altar in the city of Arezzo, one of the finest works in Italy— and one praised by all. And he also composed the book on perspective which is found in the excellent library of the Duke of Urbino."

E DIVINA PROPORTIONE, as it was printed by Paganini, gives us Pacioli's alphabet following the treatise on the solids which forms the conclusion of the text. It is not printed at the beginning, as Luca says, but as the appendix of the treatise on the proportions of the human body, etc. It is to be regretted that, garrulous as he is, Fra Luca's interest in the lettering of the ancients did not tempt him to discuss in some detail the history of its revival by the scholars and archaeologists of his own period. He only hints that the ancient habit of affixing metal-cut letters upon columns, etc., had brought to light the fact that always two lines, one curved and the other straight, "suffice for all things which have to be made in their [i.e. the letter-makers'] art." But he does not tell us, for example, whether scholars deduced the mathematical basis of classical letter from the form of the letters themselves or from the circular or other guiding indications and marks on the stones —a point to which we shall return shortly.

This is the more unfortunate as nothing explicit has descended to us—either by Vitruvius' hand, or any other— enabling us to reconstruct with precision the methods which the old Romans employed in drawing and cutting their inscriptions. According to the most authoritative of modern students of epigraphy, Emil Hübner, it is obvious that the more elegant inscriptions were drawn or painted with the aid of rule and compass. It could hardly be otherwise, for the construction of letters according to definite proportions would necessarily follow the use made of geometry in the planning of buildings; and, although to draw a fine letter by freehand is easy if the scale is small, the making, so as to look agreeable at a distance, of a word whose letters are more than a foot high is no easy matter even with instruments. The bigger the scale, the more necessary become the geometrical aids. Hence the rules for letter-making which the ancient builders used were not developed by, or even taught to, or published, in the interests of calligraphers, but concerned exclusively architects, painters and carvers. Hence the several mentions of such a matter in Luca de Pacioli's *De Divina Proportione* are perfectly appropriate, since his book is addressed to stone-cutters and builders. And, of course, as he is only concerned to indicate the method from his own point of view, he rightly abstains from providing any historical data of no strict relevance. We must rather congratulate ourselves that, instead of words, the writer gave us the magnificent blocks which it is the purpose of this work to reproduce and these preliminary pages to introduce.

If the Friar had mentioned inscriptions of his own time constructed by this method, we should have been grateful; if his, on the whole diffuse and gossipy, account had been a little more explicit he need not have suffered the taunt of Geofroy Tory that he had stolen the designs; if he had traced the efforts of any immediate predecessors in the same line of enquiry we should have been in a position to present a more satisfactory background to the history of letter carving in general and to the Friar's efforts in particular.

Tory's accusation never had any foundation. Apart from the light it may throw upon this accusation, it will be well to point out that there were writings on the same subject which antedated both Leonardo and Luca. The fact is that although Pacioli's capitals are larger in scale and more explicit in detail than those of his predecessors, the geometrical method had been published in print a quarter of a century before the year 1509 when the completed text of *De Divina Proportione* was published; and, further, that the method was already well known to classicists of still earlier days is proved by the existence in the Vatican of a manuscript model book, with instructions. The compiler of this earliest known manual was a literary man with a taste for archaeology. Like most of his kind, Felice Feliciano of Verona wrote a very decent hand of the kind we call humanistic. He even wrote out a few manuscripts in a good book-script, though more given to the current semi-formal italic in which was written the little book he dedicated *Pictorum principi ac unico lumini et cometae: magnique ingenii viro Andreae Mantegnae patauo amicorum splendori Foelix Foelicianus veronensis salutem,* a compilation of epigrams which he had copied from old inscriptions, drawings of such stones, sketches of the letters and of carved figures. Feliciano was an intimate of Mantegna and, in his company, collected the inscriptions. The drawings are carefully, but not professionally, made. The same criticism may be applied to the alphabet which the same scholar drew and which is, so far as we know, the earliest statement of the mathematical principles underlying the roman alphabet in its best lapidary form.

Feliciano appears to take the credit for the discovery, for he says, *et questo e quanto per misura io Felice Felic. ha nelle antique caractere ritrouato per molte pietre marmoree cossi nel alma Roma quanto negli altri* [*siti?*], i.e. "and this is what I, Felice Feliciano, have found by measuring the ancient characters on many marbles both at Rome and in other places." The alphabet of Feliciano concludes with formulae for making gold, silver, green, red and black colours, for making inks and varnishes.

The Vatican codex, which seems to be the original, ends with a Latin epigram dated Venice, 1481. It is surprising that Feliciano seems never to have persuaded anybody to print it for him. Or did he succeed in doing so and the book is now "lost"? It is not impossible that a copy may turn up. That a slim pamphlet of this kind easily disappears is proved by Signor L.S. Olschki's discovery of the booklet *Impressum parme per Damianum Moyllum: Parmensem*. This unique copy of an alphabet with letters cut on wood, with geometrical instructions, was recovered as lately as 1924. The work has no title-page, the colophon is undated. Our available information of Damiano da Moille was brought together in 1918 by Signor Laudedeo Testi, who found that he came from a family of calligraphers and proves that he himself practised the craft by discovering in a Graduale written for the Benedictines of Parma an initial signed DAMIANVS MOYLLVS PARMENSIS, in large classic capitals of the antique style. This manuscript is dated 1486. In his quality as a printer Damiano is known to have issued only three books: (1) a folio Graduale printed in partnership with Bernardus Moyllus in 1477, (2) a folio text of J. de Magistri's *Questiones*

in 1481, and (3) a work of similar character, N. de Orbelli's
Expositio Logicae in 1483. In all probability Damiano printed
his alphabet not long before 1477 or after 1483, i.e. more or
less contemporaneously with Feliciano's work. If we accept
the Vatican codex dated 1481 as the first appearance of his
alphabet it is possible that he was anticipated by Moille. As,
however, it is known that Feliciano's interest in inscriptions
dates back to 1463 when he travelled with Mantegna, it is not
unlikely that the Vatican codex is a late copy. As Moille's
book is printed on one side of the sheet it is possible that loose
pages were handed round in class by a master of lettering. The
absence of a title-page in spite of the available blank leaf at the
beginning points to some such extracommercial purpose. It
is possible, though unlikely, that Damiano da Moille was the
author as well as the printer of the work—the existence of a
colophon proves that he signed his work as a printer, and his
name, as Signor Testi shows, appears in one of the initials of
a choir-book written out by him. If Damiano was the author
as well as the printer of the book, it seems likely that he would
have mentioned the fact in his colophon.

The probability is that Damiano da Moille printed the book
for an author, who was perhaps a teacher of some branch of
architecture. As there is no trace of any connexion between
Feliciano and Parma, the speculation that he may have been
the author is barren. Moreover, the correspondences between
the texts of Feliciano and Moille are inconsiderable. I conclude
then that these two documents are independent.

But a comparison of the texts of Moille and Pacioli exhibits
too many instances of verbal similarity to admit of independence. Nor is it likely that Pacioli was the author of Moille's
publication, since, as far as we know, he had no connexions
with Parma and would certainly have mentioned the fact in
the epistle to his friends in the Borgo had he engaged previously
in a work of this kind. As there can be no doubt that Moille's

pamphlet came out in the 1480's I conclude that Pacioli had access to it, or to another treatise of which Moille's print was a copy. In other words, the probability is that, by the time Pacioli wrote his treatise for the benefit of his friends in the Borgo, scholars in such centres as Florence, Venice and Milan were already familiar with several manuscript opuscula, deriving no doubt, from one or two scholars of whom Feliciano is the type. That the classical capitals were very deliberately taken as models by craftsmen much earlier than the date on the manuscript of Feliciano and the printed book of Moille is proved by the very fine medals of Lysippus the Younger. Before his day, the scribes and medallists practised a majuscular script based directly upon tenth- and eleventh-century exemplars which had in them only a reminiscence of their own classical origin. One of the earliest of the humanists, Poggio, wrote, as early as 1408, a very fine hand (we should be justified in calling it early humanistic) whose capitals obviously descend from the slim florentine bastarda. At that time no scholar had shown any sign of reproducing the pure inscriptional forms of the old *scriptura monumentalis*. But it could only be a matter of time before devoted imitators of the antique civilisation fixed upon the majestic roman capitals as models for their own lettering, and thus, in the next generation, goldsmiths and other handicraftsmen led the way afterwards followed by the architects. Of course the necessarily smaller scale in which the medallists worked forbade the use of instrumental aids in the cutting of capitals. Nevertheless, it is clear that the text on such a medal as that of Raffaello Maffei da Volterra, the papal scriptor, is based upon the old stone letters. The historian of the Italian medallists definitely describes its inscriptions as "very fine monumental lettering." This medal was cut between 1466 and 1476, according to the same authority. See No. 797 in Sir George Hill's *A Corpus of Italian Medals of the Renaissance*, London, 1930.

Moreover, there is preserved in Munich an alphabet of classical capitals geometrically drawn by the German humanist, Hartmann Schedel. The details of the instructions, though by no means identical with those of Moille, are such as might be accounted for by a distant relationship to the printed original, or to an unknown earlier text. As the Schedel codex is not dated, it is impossible to discuss its position in the relation to the other existing books. But that interest in the geometry of lettering was widely spread is testified to by a very interesting anonymous codex in the possession of Mr Lindsay Ricketts of Chicago, also undated. The Ricketts manuscript deserts the method of the square and circle in favour of an alternative geometrical scheme based upon the units related to a perpendicular. It is the more unfortunate that this work is undated, for it strikes the present writer as being possibly written at an earlier date than those of Hartmann Schedel, of Damiano Moille, even of Felice Feliciano himself. The absence of data makes speculation hopeless, but the provision in the Ricketts manuscript of the geometrical regulations in the typical Florentine gothic cursive seems to indicate an origin not much later than the middle of the fifteenth century, before many humanists had adopted the new cursive used in the Papal Chancery. The present stage of our knowledge permits us only to be certain of the alphabets of which the date or the author's name is embodied in the document itself.

Thus there were at least two principal versions of the geometrical alphabet current before the publication of Pacioli's capitals, Feliciano's in manuscript and Moille's in type. Several printed versions appeared later. In 1514 Sigismondo dei Fanti of Ferrara applied the geometrical method to the (then called "moderna") round gothic letter and to the lower case as well as to the capitals. Francesco Torniello of Milan brought out a set of rules for roman capitals in 1517, and Giambattista Verini's book containing a similar set was published in 1526.

Dürer's *Unterweysung*, the first outside Italy, appeared in the previous year at Nuremberg. None of these mentions Pacioli.

Geofroy Tory's *Champ Fleury* was published in Paris in 1529. He says a good word for Dürer: "the noble German painter, who is greatly to be praised," for he has "so well set forth his art of painting by drawing the figures of Geometry, Fortifications and the Proportions of the Human Body. He is worthy to be held in immortal memory." Tory's paragraph on the Friar is in the contrary sense. He insists that "Frere Lucas Paciol of Bourg Sainct Sepulchre, of the order of Freres Mineurs, and a theologian, who has written in vulgar Italian a book entitled *Diuina Proportione* and who has essayed to draw the Attic letters, says nothing about them, nor gives explanations; and I am not surprised, for I have heard from some Italians that he purloined the said letters from the late Messire Leonardo da Vinci, who died recently at Amboise, and who was a most excellent philosopher and admirable painter and, as it were, another Archimedes. This Frere Lucas has had Leonardo's Attic letters printed as his own. In truth, they may well be his, for he has not drawn them in their proper proportions, as I shall show hereafter in treating of the said letters in their order. Nor does Sigismund Fante, a noble Ferrarian, who teaches how to write many sorts of letters, give explanations; and the like is true of Messire Ludovico Vicentino. I do not know whether Albert Dürer explains his theories; but, however that may be, he has gone astray in the proper proportions of the designs of many letters in his book on Perspective."

Thus Geofroy Tory disposes of each of his predecessors and their methods. The "graceful and elegant banquet" which he made for his readers was neither polite nor just to those who loved the antique alphabet no less surely than himself.

◆{ 4 }◆

LUCA is censured by Tory for requiring *la gamba da man drita vol esser gross a dele nove parti luna de lalteza.* This was due to the Friar's "ignorance." Dürer's "ignorance" was condoned because he was a painter. Fanti was also criticised. Nor did Ludovico Arrighi escape. Yet Tory's only important point is that he believed in a *tenth,* and not in a *ninth* unit. To understand what this means we must attend more closely than we have yet needed to the central ideas of the classical scheme as reconstructed by Feliciano, Moille, and Pacioli.

The two foundation elements common to these three early

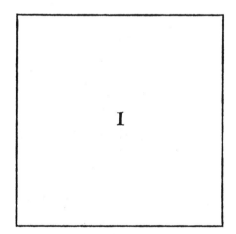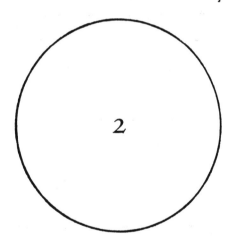

writers are the square as in 1 and the circle as in 2. These elements are next imposed as in 3; and twice bisected diagonally in 4 and then twice diametrically in 5.

According to Feliciano "the ancient usage was to make the character A from a circle and a square, the height of which ascends to LII (*sic*), whereof is formed the perfect number, which is X; and thus the thickness of the letter must be the Xth part of its height," etc.; throughout his method Feliciano consistently requires the thick stem of his letters to be one-tenth the measure of its height. Why he mentions LII (= 52) instead of L (= 50) is not clear; unless he means that the apex of the A should extend two points over the height of the square we must regard LII as intended for L. But Feliciano's important point is his insistence upon the thickness of the

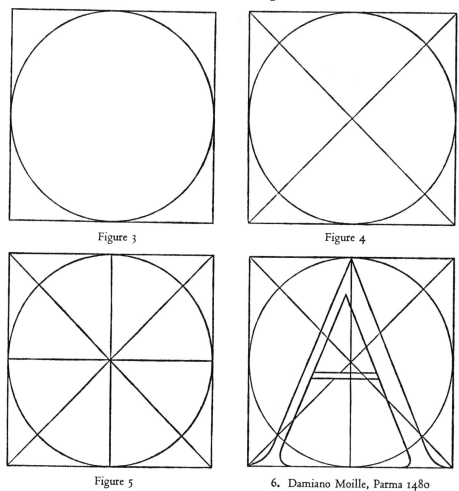

Figure 3

Figure 4

Figure 5

6. Damiano Moille, Parma 1480

stem being one-tenth of the height of the square. Moille, on the other hand, says that the thickness of the mainstroke should be one-twelfth of its height. Pacioli states that "the right limb [of A] must be one-ninth part as thick as the height." Dürer deserts him, for he instructs his readers to "draw for each [letter] a square of uniform size, in which each letter is to be contained. But when you draw in it the heavier limb of the letter, make this of the width of one-tenth part of the square ....'' Although Dürer elected to use the tenth part he in no way condemns those who followed the

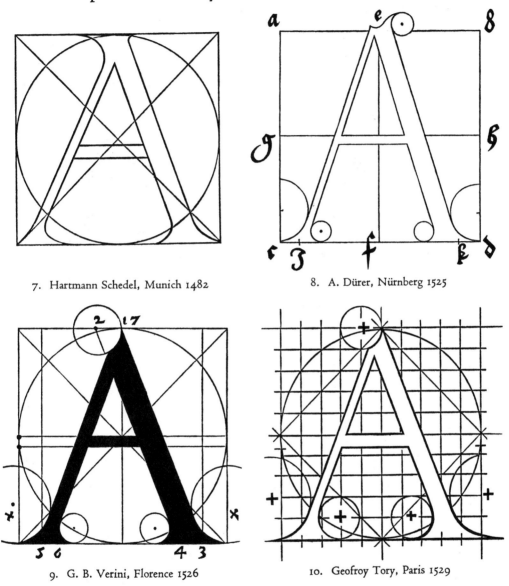

7. Hartmann Schedel, Munich 1482

8. A. Dürer, Nürnberg 1525

9. G. B. Verini, Florence 1526

10. Geofroy Tory, Paris 1529

earlier rule, although he must have been aware of Pacioli's publication. Unlike Tory, Dürer's mind was free from theoretical prejudices and he could look tolerantly upon the use of the ninth, tenth or twelfth measures. Dürer however makes less constant use than Moille or Pacioli of the compass, as may be seen from his method of making the roman A in figure 8. That the compass was still used in Italy in Dürer's time for making the roman A may be seen in figure 9 which is taken from G. B. Verini's book of 1526.

Tory, though following Dürer in important respects, is dogmatically bound to the use of the circle as well as the square. But he carries the whole idea a step farther: he sub-cuts the field into squares by dividing the horizontals and the perpendiculars

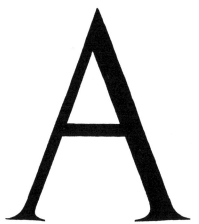 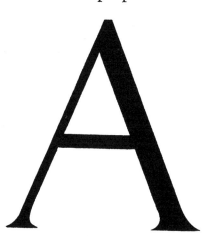

11. Dürer, 1525   12. Urban Wyss, Nürnberg 1553

into ten equal portions as in figure 10. Apart from Tory's insistence upon the importance of his cabalistic abracadabra and his use of a field cut into a hundred equal squares, his whole practical difference from the Friar, who taught a ratio of 1 : 9, is that he demands letters where mainstrokes shall be one-tenth their height. There can be no greater example of shibboleth, for, in spite of the applicability of the system to inscriptions on pillars and architraves, where the capitals would be of maximum size, the general mass of letter-cutters were necessarily occupied with work on a smaller scale, e.g. inscriptions on tombs and walls in which the lettering did not exceed 3 or 4 inches in height—the measure, in fact, of the blocks which the Friar annexed to the *De Divina Proportione*. The difference between a letter whose main stem is one-tenth, and another one-twelfth the thickness of the square does not affect the essentials of the design, and therefore does not materially affect the appearance of the resulting inscription, as the two cuts below suffice to prove. Tory's prejudice was on the side of a thickness of letter equal to one-tenth of its height for the —to him sufficient—reason that there were Nine Muses, and Apollo a tenth. He habitually uses the Compass and the Rule because he is convinced that they are the King and Queen respectively of instruments. It follows that Tory judges a roman

13. The Thick Leg in the above is $\frac{1}{9}$ of the height   14. The Thick Leg here is $\frac{1}{10}$ of the height

letter by the method of its construction and not by its appearance; and, moreover, he judges a method by its congruity or otherwise with his deductions from the classical myths. If Dürer was a practical artist, and Tory was a mystagogue, Pacioli was a rationalist.

It may be justly claimed, therefore, for Pacioli's alphabet that it is as practical as Tory's; and rather more so, since in making his capitals he disregards any other than the purely objective considerations. The scale of the Friar's diagrams gives them a considerable advantage, and the simplicity of his field, as contrasted with Tory's insistence upon sub-dividing it into 100 component squares, is greatly in its favour.

Before leaving Tory we ought perhaps to say a word on the accusation he levels at Pacioli's honesty. We have already mentioned Luca's honesty in giving credit to Leonardo da Vinci and to Pietro degli Franceschi. Geofroy Tory's statements of the Friar that *il a derobé les dictes lettres* and that *il a prins secrettement* are, he himself says, based on what he "had heard from some Italians." This hearsay was probably derived from irresponsible studio-gossips; but that Tory's bias is due to sheer pride is obvious from his determination to quarrel not only with the work of the dead Friar, but with work of the same kind by anybody else. Finally, Tory's reference to his "having heard from some Italians" that the Friar's letters were stolen from Leonardo, reminds one of a passage in Vasari's Life of Pietro degli Franceschi. Vasari, who was a native of Arezzo, either invented or retailed a story which was no doubt current at the time when the Friar, like other distinguished contemporaries, had his detractors.

Although Vasari's book was not published until 1550, what he says was possibly current among an earlier generation of gossips. Vasari goes further and overreaches himself when he says that Fra Luca del Borgo was so envious that he did his utmost to annihilate the name of Pietro, his instructor, and sought to arrogate to himself honours due to his teacher alone. He even, says Vasari, "published, under his own name, all the laborious works of that good old man." Of course there is no sort of justification for this statement, as may be seen from the books themselves. And on the contrary, the Friar names Piero in the text of *De Divina Proportione* as the "sovereign contemporary master of painting and architecture." It is difficult to imagine a more generous tribute.

With so much by way of preface, it is now time to turn to the reproduction of the Friar's capitals. When the reader has inspected these, we shall offer in a postscript a few words on the designs as they strike the modern eye.

PACIOLI's ALPHABET

This letter is taken from the circle and square.
The right limb must be one-ninth part as thick
as the height. The left limb is to be half as thick
as the thick one. The middle [cross-] limb is
to be one-third of the thickness of the thick
limb. Of the said letter, the middle limb—the
breadth of the letter [between] each limb—
lies a little lower than the junction [of the dia-
gonals] as you see by the diameters indicated.

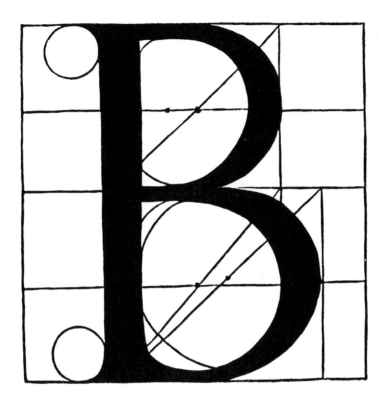

This letter is made of two circles together, of which the lower one is the larger; namely, its diameter must be five-ninths of the total height, as is seen indicated in due proportion above.

This letter is taken from the circle and its
square, thickening the fourth part both outside
and inside [curve of the circle]. The upper
limb ends at the point of intersection of the
diameter and circumference, the lower passes
over the crossing about half a ninth near the
corner of the square, as is shown in the figure,
and it is made in the same way as O.

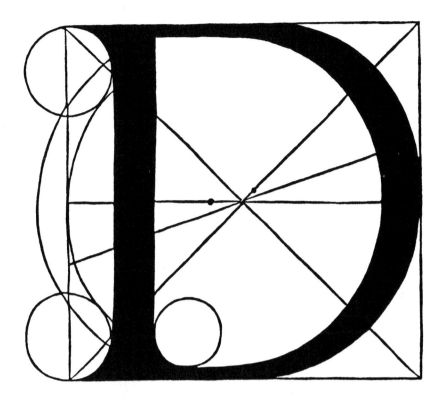

This letter is taken from the circle and a square.
The straight limb must be one-ninth part thick
between the crossings [of the circle and diago-
nals]. The body is thickened as in the other
curves. The connecting portion at the top must
be one-third as thick as the thick limb; that
at the bottom a fourth more than a third.

35

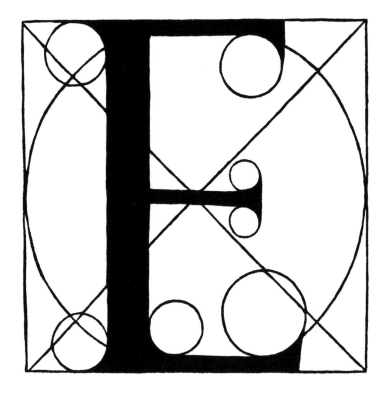

This letter is produced from the circle and its square. The thick limb must be one-ninth part. The upper limb must be one-half the thickness of the thick limb, the lower limb likewise; the middle limb the third part of the thick limb, like the middle [limb] of A, and the letter must be as wide as one-half the square, and so it will be most perfect.

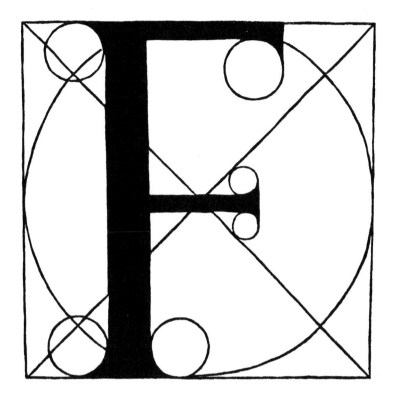

This letter is made like E, neither more nor less, save that F has no third limb; as you will find more fully set forth under E, with all its due proportions, so that this suffices for this letter.

This letter G is made like C from its circle and
square. The straight limb at the bottom must
be one-third of the square in height, and its
thickness one-ninth of the height of the square.

This letter is made from the circle and its square; the thick limbs are made through the crossing, that is, where the diameters of the circle and square intersect each other. The thickness of the said limbs must be one-ninth of the height; the middle limb is made through the diameter, its thickness being one-third of that of the thick limbs, like the crossbar of the A.

This letter is made from the circle and square, and its thickness must be one-ninth; so that it is easier to make than the others.

This letter is made from the circle and the
square, drawing a line through the diameter of
the square, on which line the two limbs are ter-
minated and joined in the middle of the thick
limb. The lower limb must be one-ninth in
thickness like the other limbs; the upper limb
one-half the thickness of the thick limb, as with
the left limb of A. The lower limb must be long
enough to reach the intersection [of the dia-
gonals] and the circle, or more; the upper one
ends short of the intersection.

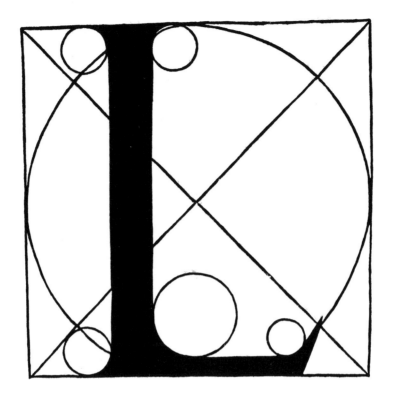

This letter is formed from the circle and square.
Its thickness must be one-ninth of its height;
its width the half of the square, with the round-
ings (*tondi*) inscribed above. The thin limb at
the bottom must be half the thickness of the
thick limb, as with E and F.

This letter is made from the circle and its square.
The thin limbs must be half the thickness of the
thick ones, like the left limb of A. The outer
limbs must be slightly inside the square; the
middle limbs between them and the intersection
of the diameter, their width, both the thick and
the thin, like those of the A, as you may see
more clearly in the figure.

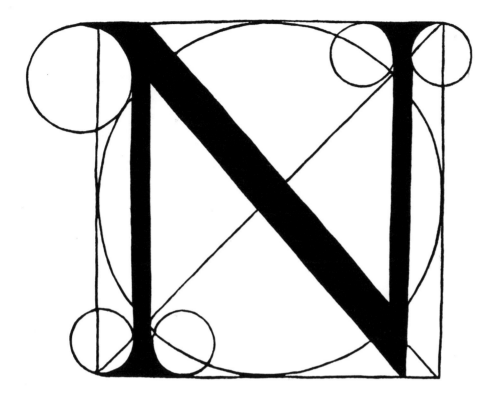

This letter is made from the circle and square.
The first limb must fall beyond the intersection
of the diagonals [and circle]. The middle limb
must be one-ninth in thickness, taken diagonally. The third limb must fall outside the intersection. The first and third limbs must be half
as thick as the thick limb, that is, one head [or
one-ninth].

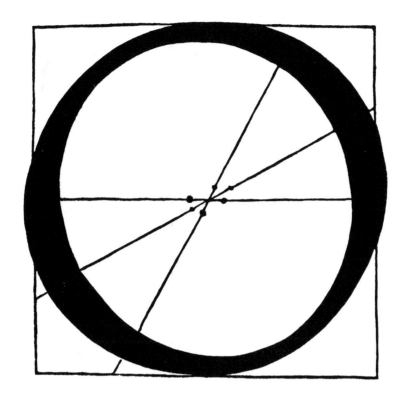

This O is most perfect.

[The second design for O, shown on page 57, gives a description which almost seems more satisfactory if transferred to this first O which Pacioli terms *perfectissimo*. The protuberances (*pancie*) are more conspicuously swung "one upwards, the other downwards" in the above. Hence it is possible that there was some confusion in the setting of the text. It would appear more reasonable to reverse the positions of these two designs, but I have retained the order of the original. Cf. the Q, pp. 60 and 61. S.M.]

This letter is made from the circle and its square. It is divided into four parts, that is, crosswise by the four middle lines. Its body must be one-ninth thick, and its upper part must be half the thickness of the thick part. Its protuberances must lie one upwards, the other downwards; the thin parts of its body must be one-third of the protuberance. And seeing that there are two opinions about it, I have provided another which in my view is most perfect; and you can take which you like, and form from it, as you will find set out in its place.

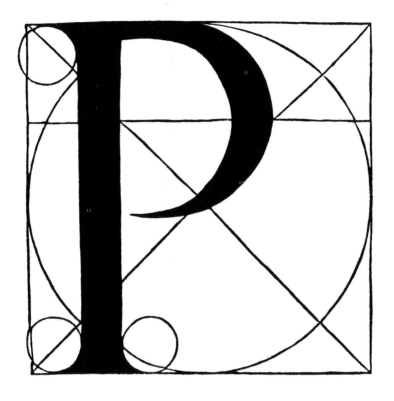

This letter is taken from the circle and its square. Its thick limb must be one-ninth in thickness. The shape of the round part must be as large as the lower part of B, and the thickness of the protuberance must be as great as the thick limb, and the said letter must begin at the crossing of the great circle, that is, the intersection of the diameter, and thus it will be most perfect.

[The tail of the Q in the engraving ends nearly four heads or ninths below the square. Hence the design does not appear in the stated proportions. The tail of the Q in the engraving is longer than the side of the square. It will be noted that the Friar shows here the alternative O instead of the *perfectissimo*. Cf. pp. 55 and 57. S.M.]

This letter, as I said above,
is made from the O, its limb
ending three heads of its height below the square, that is, three-ninths of
the square, or the diameter of the circle, as here
appears in due proportion, keeping the thick
and thin protuberances opposite each other as
was said in the case of O. Its tail is to be made
nine heads long, that is, as long as the side of
its square; and the head must be one-ninth of
the height high at the point, following the curve
of the pen with the lessening of its thickness.

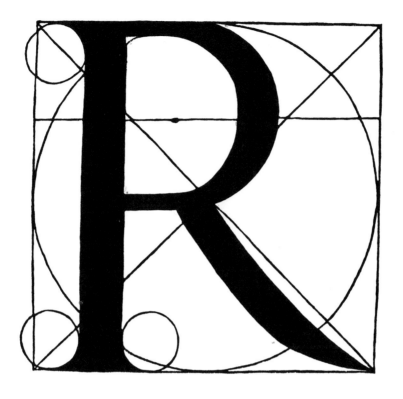

This letter is taken from B, its rounding extends to a half [thick] limb below the centre. The whole of this letter must be within the intersections except the curved limb, which must pass beyond the intersections to the corner of the square. The said curved leg is to be one-ninth thick, ending thinly in a point at the angle of the square after the manner of curved lines, as you see from the illustration.

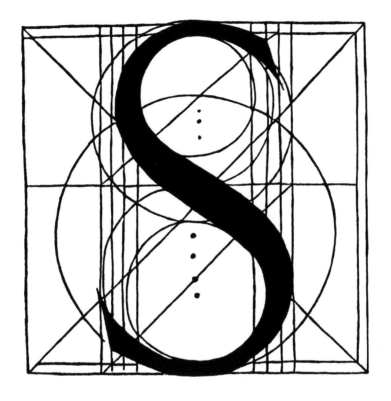

This letter is made from eight [the figure gives only six] circles, and this is its mode of formation, as you see in the figure. Finding their centres by means of their parallels, you will find that those below are one-third of one-ninth of the square greater than those above. The protuberance at the middle must be one-ninth of the height; the thin portions a third of the thickness, ending the heads with their ornament (*con sua gratia*).

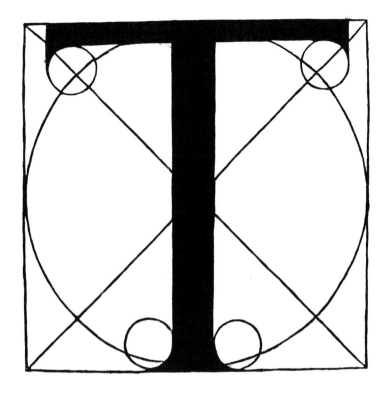

This letter is made from the circle and square. The thick limb must be made exactly as we said of I. The cross limb must be half as thick as the thick limb, as in the cases of E and F above, and must end half a head from the corner of the square on both sides, and thus it will be most pleasing to the eye.

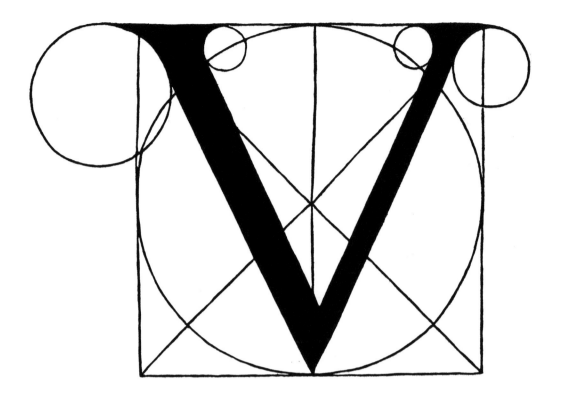

This letter is made from the whole square. The
left limb must be one-ninth [the height] of the
square in thickness, taken diagonally, like the
right limb of A and the cross limb of N, the
right limb half the thick one taken diagonally,
like the left limb of A, and it ends in a point
at the base of the square at the end of the diameter of the circle.

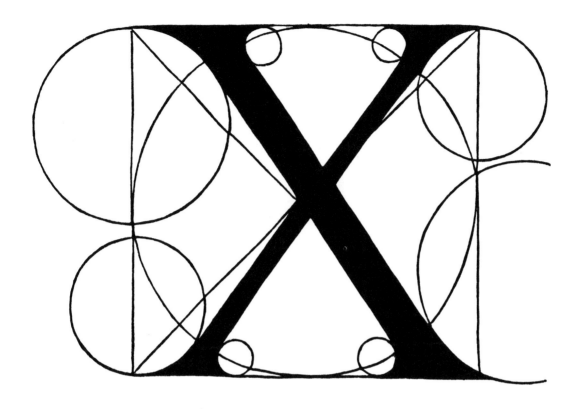

This letter requires the whole square, its limbs crossing at the intersection of the diameters. And the one must be one-ninth of the height in thickness; the other half this [thickness], taken diagonally, its limbs ending with the requisite grace under the control of the small circles.

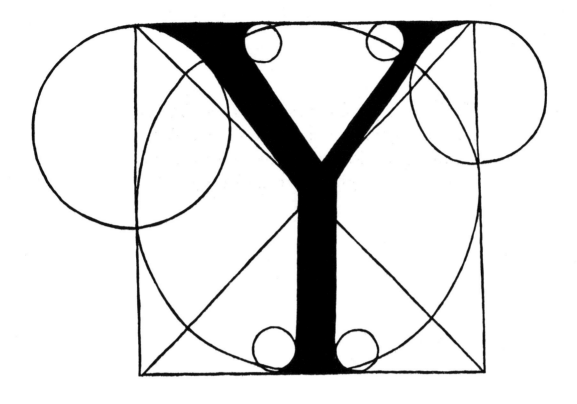

This letter makes use of the whole square; the right and left limbs must be thick in the same proportion as those of V, save that they end exactly above the intersection of the diameters, and thence their junction, produced downwards to the base of the square, is one-ninth of the square in thickness; the upper heads end with their own circles, as you see.

[The Y is the final letter in *De Divina Propor-tione*. The Friar naturally ignores U and W but the omission of Z seems to be due to accident. Z is given by Moille, Dürer and Tory. S.M.]

POSTSCRIPT

⚔ POSTSCRIPT ☙

ERY few of us, familiar as we are with the description "Roman Letter"— and the thing itself—understand at first why a thing so simple to look at should be so difficult to make, and above all, why it should be considered necessary to erect a geometrical scaffolding with □ ○ ⊠ ⊞ and ▦ in support of an obviously simple construction. Yet simple as the A B C looks we all know it is difficult because we have all tried at one time or another to make a set of capitals, or at least to write our name out in what customs and other officials describe as "block" letters. A better and more admirable term would be "roman." Another term used in official circles is "print"—a permissible if not an admirable term. But "roman" or "print" or "block," the making of even a tolerably decent alphabet is not so easy as it looks, in spite of the fact that rule and compass are not really required, except by workmen engaged in large-scale letter-cutting. The rest of us govern our hands with our eyes, and when we are asked to make a set of capitals we set down, as nearly as we can, the alphabet of the printer.

The most conspicuous difference between the lettering derived from the old roman *scriptura monumentalis* and the upper-case used by present-day printers is in the extension of several characters which, according to the classical letter-cutters and their disciples of the Renaissance, occupied half a square. If the curious will compare the letters B, E, F, K, L, P, S with the other letters of the alphabet, he will find that they look narrower, and even conspicuously narrower. The only cause forthcoming for this difference in measure is the difference in form: it was felt that the nature of the shapes of B and S, for example, essentially required a narrower measure than the square which M clearly demands. The letter S, extended to a square in the so-called Lombard style, would have been regarded in classic times as a barbarity; and in fact it was so regarded by the renaissance scholars responsible for bringing writing and printing back to the classical sources of inspiration. It does not follow, however, that if B and S must be less square than M they need be half the square in measure; yet many excellent roman sculptors seem to have considered the half square the best proportion for E, F, S, etc. There exist numerous inscriptions with wide E, but wide S never appears. The general, almost invariable, custom in the *scriptura monumentalis* was to make the short bars to the E of equal length thus: E. The writers of the renaissance including Pacioli departed from the classical exemplars by varying the length of the bars and recommending sculptors to extend the base beyond the length of the upper bars. In the course of time the centre became much shorter than the remaining bars.

This was a natural development, for the necessities of architects and sculptors, though analogous, are not identical with those of punch-cutters and printers. Having learned and memorised the true proportions of roman letter as taught in the manuals of Moille, Pacioli and others, the goldsmiths, punch-cutters and printers relied on their eyes and not upon their measuring tools. The calligraphers were of the same mind. Hence, even in the renaissance period itself, the construction of roman capitals in absolute conformity with classical precedents is exceptional either in written codices or in printed books. There could be no point in the use of the rule and compass in lettering much smaller in scale than the blocks shown in the preceding introduction. The blocks used in Moille are cut on a square slightly over $2\frac{1}{2}''$, perhaps the minimum size allowing easy manipulation of the tools. Even in this size, however, it would be quite possible for a true craftsman to draw the characters free hand. But the mass of printing in roman type in fifteenth-century Venice, Florence, Rome and elsewhere was composed in founts whose capitals were not based even at second hand upon the models circulated by Feliciano, Pacioli or Moille. Although not always very literally, the bulk of the roman capitals used by fifteenth-century printers derive from titles employed in the books of that earlier Renaissance which Charlemagne had directed in the eighth century. Thus, Jenson's capitals are by no means immediately classical; they descend from Caroline models. Although these models were themselves based upon roman they are squarer and bolder forms than those of the original inscriptions: in fact they are freely drawn broad-pen versions of the *scriptura monumentalis*. There was, then, only limited use of the strictly classical models in fifteenth-century printing centres.

There was one powerful exception at the end of the century. Aldus Manutius Romanus secured a set of punches from Francesco Griffo of Bologna which are obviously cut upon classical lines. The Griffo fount was first used in 1495. Aldus, who planned to publish editions of Greek and Latin authors, brought out in that year a dialogue which Pietro Bembo had written in the style of Sallust. It seems likely that Aldus instructed his punch-cutter to follow classical models. At least the capitals which Griffo cut more nearly approach the *scriptura monumentalis* than any other in the century. Its faithful adherence to Rome is manifested in the orthodoxy of its E. The size of the original type is that usual in the Venice of that day. I have never seen small types cut in accordance with the classical rules except the capitals to Arrighi's second italic of 1523. This fount possesses the orthodox E with bars of equal length. Of course Griffo's and Arrighi's forms were never

geometrically laid out : inasmuch as printing types are necessarily small, their lines depend strictly upon the engraver's
visual and manual skill in following a model, in this case evidently an orthodox set of classical capitals.

A B C D E F G H I J K L M N
O P Q R S T U V W X Y Z

The alphabet (enlarged) according to the proportions of Nicolas Jenson (Venice 1470)

A B C D E F G H I J K L M N
O P Q R S T U V W X Y Z

The alphabet (enlarged) according to the proportions of Aldus Manutius (Venice 1495)

Successive generations of punch-cutters and printers ad-
justed his varying shapes in order to avoid a contrast between
wide and narrow letters. In other words, whereas the old
romans and neo-classicists of the fifteenth and sixteenth centuries used an alphabet comprising a square and half a square
in measure, the later printer developed a set of characters
comprising many varieties of measure expressly to dispose of
contrast. By this means, readers have been accustomed to an
alphabet whose E and S, for example, are wider than would
have been approved by classicists. It would seem, as far as the
present-day is concerned, that there is no likelihood of any
widespread adoption of the purely classical dimensions by the
printing trade. Not since the peak of the Renaissance have
printers been influenced by the books of Moille and Pacioli.
I have mentioned Arrighi's small classical capitals. The finest
large inscriptional letters cast as type and used by any printer
known to me are those on the title-page of the superb three-
volume Bible published Romae Ex Typographia Apostolica
Vaticana (1590). Although printers in the sixteenth century
followed Aldus, or rather the letters which Griffo had cut for

him, they did not do so literally. Few cared for the narrow orthodox classical E. Jenson's E was perhaps too wide. The form approved by the majority was E. The wide distribution of books naturally brought the printed letter to the first place as the norm of the alphabet. In consequence the penmanship of later periods increasingly departs from the classical or renaissance models. It seems to have been felt, too, that small letters require thicker stems, certainly thicker than a ninth or a tenth of the height.

Thus the development in typography during the sixteenth and seventeenth centuries moved, without exception, towards an assimilation of the classical capitals as geometrically made, with the changes in scale necessitated by the reduced dimensions of which the growing technique of typographers permitted them the mastery. The smaller the letters became the less the need for the geometry and the less need for insistence upon the classical proportions; capitals became wider as the height was reduced. No doubt Nicolas Jenson saw the advisability to widen the narrow sorts while Francesco Griffo thought that this was necessary only in still smaller letters.

In calligraphy and in the applications of calligraphy which modern parlance describes as "lettering" the situation was at first slightly more favourable to the inscriptional letter. The first copybook compiled in the interest of non-professional writers and brought out by Ludovico Arrighi in 1520, set a precedent followed by two generations of writing masters by presenting students with a copy of the complete alphabet of roman letters. It seems, by the way, that the term "roman" originated at this time. Arrighi (Rome 1520) shows the capitals; Tagliente (Venice 1523) also, but Palatino seems the first (1545) to use the term "Lettere Romane" instead of "antique" or "antiqua" or "antiche" employed by Pacioli and other writers. But the roman letters given by Arrighi, though clearly classical, are put forward as the result of calligraphical, not of

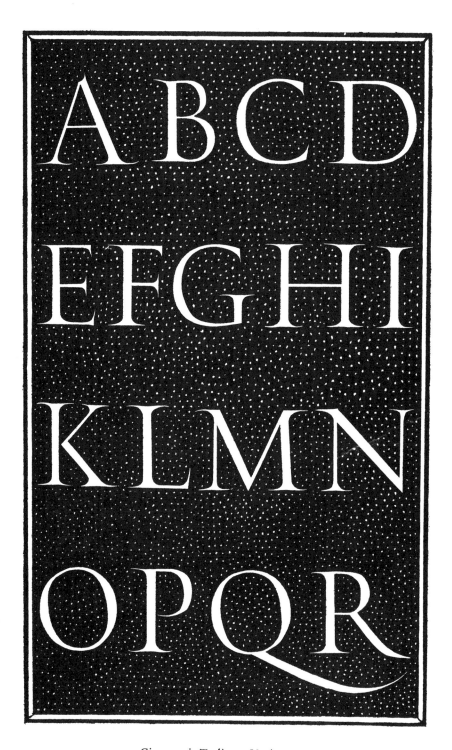

Giovantonio Tagliente, Venice 1523

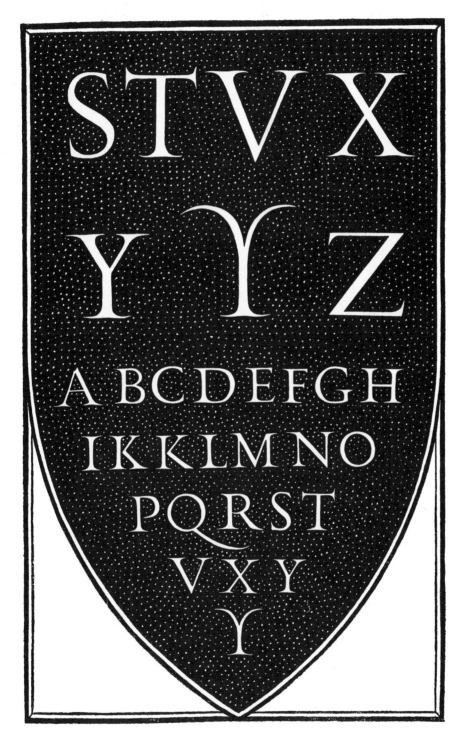

Giovantonio Tagliente, Venice 1523

geometrical skill. The models in books published by Arrighi's immediate successors, Tagliente and Palatino, follow the same lead. A Franciscan, Father Vespasiano Amphiareo, added

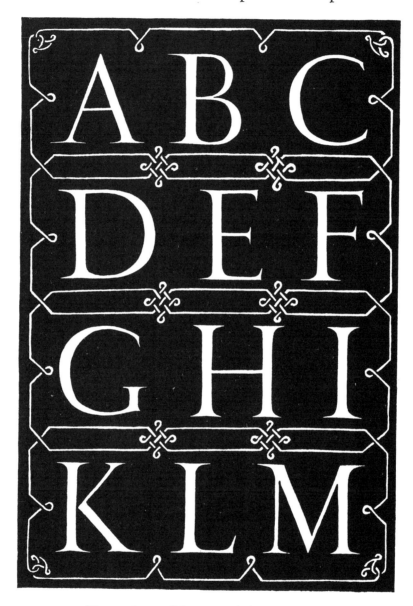

"Lettere Romane" by G. B. Palatino, Rome 1545

to his copybook, published in 1555, a set of roman letters constructed on squares cut into eighths. Later the calligraphers took to imitating the letters of printers.

Whatever the prejudices of calligraphers or typographers,

architects and sculptors viewed the old capitals differently. They were the first to imitate them and they still imitate them. There is a sarcophagus in the Church of St John Lateran dated

"Lettere Romane" by G. B. Palatino, Rome 1545

as early as 1447 carrying an inscription of six lines in classical lettering, though the forms are unseriffed. Thenceforward, architects approximated closer and closer in every detail to the antique models. It was precisely with such an intention that Pacioli wrote supplementary portions of his *De Divina Proportione* addressed to Cesare de Saxo and their companions, "worthy stone-cutters and zealous followers of the craft of sculpture and architecture," and constructed his alphabet for their inspiration. The revival of classical studies and the place taken by the classics in the education of western mankind from the Renaissance onwards have perpetuated the

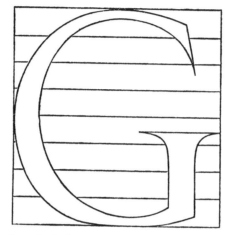

Amphiareo's method of constructing roman letters (Florence 1555)

authority of the Latin language as the timeless, universal and international medium. Conformably with this long-standing tradition, architects of permanent public edifices still choose the old roman capitals as the most consistent inscriptional alphabet. As long, therefore, as the Latin language holds its position as the international language of learning, so long will there be not merely an interest in but a use for the treatises on classical lettering such as Pacioli's.

The investigation of classical principles as they apply to lettering is, of course, a branch of the study of inscriptions, itself a branch of the study of palaeography. Scientific study of roman inscriptions was set on foot by Mommsen in 1847. His associate, Emil Hübner, produced, as part of Mommsen's corpus, his *Exempla Scripturae Epigraphica Latine*, comprising some 1200 drawings after inscriptions of the Imperial age, and preceded by an introduction to their study, unfortunately without entering, in any detail, into the question of their geometrical form. Hübner is content to remark that their construction with the rule and compass is obvious. A French scholar, Antoine Boissieu, catalogued the inscriptions of the roman period discovered in Lyons. His volume was printed with great distinction in a series of new founts, the "Caractères Augustaux" cut by the typefounder, Francis Rey, for the press of Louis Perrin. These founts, undeniably handsome, are more satisfactory in the upper-case which most strictly followed classical rules. They had no more than a local success at the time, but they caught the eye of a London scholar who persuaded the Chiswick Press to purchase strikes of the capitals. In the 1850's these were known as Lyons capitals. The most recent example of the influence upon typographers of the classical models occurs in Mr Frederic Goudy's "Forum" and "Hadriano," both admirable founts of type. It would seem that, at intervals between the invention of decorative, grotesque, or at any rate individualist, letters, printers rediscovered the authority of the simple but grand lines of the old roman. But the true old roman letters were developed by and for sculptors and so their grandeur is not seen on the page of a book. Hence, let the printer use the letters if he can—yet they are not to be judged by their utility to him. This independence of typography and calligraphy is the old roman's best title to permanence. As they are older than printing, it is safe to say that they will persist long after new methods have superseded present methods of printing, or writing.

At the present time, lettering for commercial purposes is affected by a degree of individualism more extreme than that of the pre-war generation. Indeed, we have to go back a century—to the 1820's and 1830's—for parallel examples to the grotesque shapes paradoxically known to this generation of lettering "artists" and sign writers as "modernistic."

The proper matter for the old roman letter is an inscription in the Latin language; the proper position for inscriptions is, as Fra Luca points out, on architraves and stilobates or other positions where they may instruct the public eye. Moreover, as it is not possible to imagine the learned world forgoing the exactitude and international convenience of the Latin language in favour of any new substitute, it is likely that inscriptions, at least on academic buildings, will be written in Latin and therefore carved in the letter which Fra Luca recommended to his friends in the Borgo as L'ALPHABETO DIGNISSIMO ANTICO.

BIBLIOGRAPHY

BIBLIOGRAPHICAL NOTES ON THE WORKS OF LUCA DE PACIOLI

BY PHILIP HOFER

COMPRISED in the following list will be found the printed works, and editions, of Luca de Pacioli which, in a somewhat limited time, I have been able to see or find reported. One, *La Scuola Perfetta dei Mercanti*, is conceivably mythical. The *Euclid* is very rare indeed, and the *Divina Proportione*, in fine condition, only slightly less so. Both 1494 and 1523 editions of the *Summa de Arithmetica*, however, are available in the great public collections, although they are in no sense commonly to be met with. In making these notes, I have followed the chronological sequence in which the four works, apparently, were first published.

I A

SŪMA DE ARITHMETICA GEOMETRIA PROPORTIONE & PROPORTIONALITA: (*etc.*)

Venice: Paganinus de Paganinis, 20 November 1494. Folio ($12\frac{1}{4} \times 8\frac{1}{2}$ inches). First edition.
Collation (Part I): 8 leaves unsigned; a-z⁸; ζ^8; $\mathfrak{I}^8$; $\mathfrak{V}^{10}$; AA¹⁴ = 232 leaves.

The first general work on mathematics. (See David Eugene Smith, *Rara Arithmetica*, pp. 54-57.) Written in Italian and printed in rotunda. Title-page is without ornamentation and is

entirely printed in black. Some initial letters are ornamental,
white on black, others are omitted for the rubricator. The
text commences on a₁ recto, and has six (and a fraction) lines
printed in red. There are marginal diagrams throughout the
book, and several pages of charts including the first to repre-
sent the finger symbolism of numbers. Part I ends with a two
line colophon, "Et si sequenti p̄ti p̄ncipali Geoᵉ. finis decima
nouembris ῑpositus fuerit: huic tamen p̄ti: die vigesi/ma eius-
dem ῑpositus fuit. Mᵒ.cccc.lxliiii," etc.

Then follows Part II of this same work (without a title-
page): "Tractatus Geometrie. Pars secunda principalis hui⁹
operis & prῑo eius diuisio."

Collation (Part II): A-H⁸; I-K⁶ = 76 leaves. Total: 308
leaves in the book.

Also in Italian, printed in the same rotunda type, and with
geometrical diagrams in the margins. Those on G₄ verso and
G₅ recto have some artistic merit. Part II ends with the colophon (abbreviated): "Con spesa e diligentia...del prudente
homo Paganino de Paganini da Brescia...Vinegia...Negliāni...
M.cccc.lxliiii adi 10 de nouēbre."

Some note of the variations found in different copies of this
book should be made. I have examined only four copies, but in
all of these there are pages wrongly numbered at the top right
hand corner, and there are small differences in the actual type-
setting. For example, in one copy certain words are contracted,
while in another they are spelled out. Whether these variations
are consistent enough to denote a separate issue—or issues—
of the book is open to question. One would have to examine
a considerable number of copies, and more space would be
needed for discussion than is available here. I should like,
however, to point out one rather striking variation which,
apparently, has not hitherto been specifically noted. It may
be seen on comparing the British Museum and the Bodleian

Library copies. The former has large initial letters L, D and N on a₁ recto (the first page of text, in Part I) while the latter has no large initials, but simply guide letters—small l, d and n—left for the rubricator. The New York Public Library (De Thou-Astor) copy is like the Bodleian. For those who would pursue this subject further, see Pietro Riccardi, "Biblioteca Matematica Italiana," vol. II of Part I, pp. 227-8. Also, "Atti dell' Accademia de' Nuovi Lincei" for the year 1863, and Narducci's "Intorno a due Edizioni della Summa de Arithmetica di Frate Luca Pacioli," Rome 1862.

Five copies of this first edition of the *Sūma de Arithmetica* are reported as being in America in 1919 by Winship's "Census": New York Public Library, Professor David Eugene Smith and George A. Plimpton (New York), the Boston Public Library, and Henry Walters' Collection (Baltimore).

I B

SUMMA DE ARITHMETICA GEOMETRIA. PROPORTIONI: ET PROPORTIONALITA: *(etc.)*

Toscolano: Paganinus, 10 November-20 December 1523.
Folio ($12\frac{1}{4} \times 8\frac{1}{2}$ inches). Second edition.
Collation (Part I): 8 leaves unsigned; A-Z⁸; $\mathfrak{t}$⁸; $\mathfrak{d}$⁸; $\mathfrak{v}$¹⁰; AA¹⁴ = 232 leaves.

In Italian, printed in a thinner, slightly cursive, rotunda type. The wording on the title-page differs from that of the 1494 edition: the upper seventeen lines are printed in red ink, while the whole page is surrounded with an ornamental border of white "rope" pattern on a black ground. The text is exactly the same as in the 1494 edition, with minor changes in type-setting and typographical design. For example, there are no initial letters left for the rubricator. Capitals are either ornamental or plain and are in a later style, except for the initial L (showing the author with his book and compasses) which had been used several times in the earlier edition. Some initial letters are borrowed from the *Divina Proportione* of 1509. The decorative border used on the title is used again to surround A₁ recto. (This border, slightly modified, and some of the initials, enlarged, appear in this present publication.) Part I ends with a two line colophon, the same exactly (including the 1494 date) as in the first edition.

Then follows Part II, also with the same wording as in 1494, and without a title-page.

Collation (Part II): AA⁸; B-H⁸; I-K⁶ = 76 leaves.

Also in Italian, and printed in the same slightly cursive, roman type. The geometrical figures in the margins are taken from the 1494 edition, bodily, as is the text and the colophon. Then there is added a second colophon (four lines) which reads (abbreviated) as follows: "Et per esso paganino di nouo impressa. In Tusculano…Finita adi.xx. Decembre. 1523."

Again slight variations in different copies might be cited. Riccardi (vol. II of Part I, p. 227) refers to them, as does David Eugene Smith (p. 58). I think, however, that Professor Smith has accidently misquoted De Morgan as pointing out variations in this 1523 edition—De Morgan refers, specifically, only to the 1494 edition.

2

DIVINA PROPORTIONE OPERA A TUTTI GLINGEGNI PERSPICACI E CURIOSI NECESSARIA OVE CIASCUN STUDIOSO DI PHILOSOPHIA: (*etc.*)

Venice: Paganinus, 1 June 1509.
Folio (11½ × 7¾ inches). Only edition.
Collation (Part I): A⁶; B-D⁸; E¹⁰ = 40 leaves.

Diuina

proportione

Opera a tutti glingegni perſpi
caci e curioſi neceſſaria Oue cia
ſcun ſtudioſo di Philoſophia:
Proſpectiua Pictura Sculptu
ra: Architectura: Muſica: e
altre Mathematice: ſua
uiſſima: ſottile: e ad
mirabile doctrina
conſequira: e de
lectaraſſi:cóua
rie queſtione
de ſecretiſſi
ma ſcien
tia.

M. Antonio Capella er uditiſſ. recenſente:
A. Paganius Paga ninus Characteri
bus elegantiſſimis accuratiſsi
me imprimebat.

In Italian, printed in a slightly cursive roman type, resembling but different from that used in the *Summa de Arithmetica* of 1523. The type is generally smaller face. The first two lines of the title are printed in red, beginning with an ornamental initial D (white rope pattern, on a criblé ground). More initials of this style, and a few white vine style, occur throughout the text. Part I ends with a six line colophon, as follows (abbreviated): "Venetiis Impressum per…Paganinum de paganinis de Briscia…Anno…M.D.IX. klen. Iunii," *etc.* Signature E_{10} is blank.

Then follows Part II (without a title-page) as follows: "Libellus in tres partiales diuisus" *etc.*, printed and ornamented exactly as Part I. It also ends with the same colophon as noted (in abbreviated form) under Part I. The verso of signature c_{10} is blank.

Collation (Part II): a-b^8; c^{10} = 26 leaves.

Parts III and IV have no title-pages and no text, except that which is given in explanation of the figures on the recto of each page. These explanations are printed in roman type. The verso of each page is blank. There are no signature marks in either part and there are no numbers to the leaves in Part III, which are in consequence frequently misbound.

Part III would seem most properly to consist of one page with a woodcut diagram of a human head, in profile, geometrically constructed, and the words "Diuina" and "Proportio" to the left and right respectively at the top of the page. Then follow the twenty-three letters of the alphabet (two O's and no Z) which form the main theme of this book. An architectural woodcut of an arch and two pages of illustrations of architectural terms complete this section of the book. Total: 27 leaves, in Part III.

Part IV consists of 59 numbered leaves (lettered LXI), each showing a different solid geometrical woodcut figure, with brief explanation in Greek and in Latin, and one final leaf, a chart "Arbor Proportio et Proportionalitas" printed in black and red, in roman type. The verso of this leaf, too, is blank. There is no final colophon. Total, Part IV, 60 leaves; the whole book, 153 leaves.

Obviously, with so many pages unsigned there are many variations as to the order of binding. The above seems to me, however, to be the most logical. There are also variations in printing which Riccardi (p. 229) carefully lists, but the four copies which I have examined have more and different variation. I have not myself seen any such important variation as the first ornamental initial D on the title in black instead of in red, but Mr A. F. Johnson reports that the British Museum copies both vary in this particular. An exceptional copy of this work, in contemporary binding, from which the facsimiles of the alphabet in this book are taken, measures nearly the same size as the *Summa de Arithmetica*. It is not illogical to suppose, then, that originally the books were the same dimensions. But no other copy that I have seen, or found reported, of the *Divina Proportione* is nearly so large.

3

EUCLIDIS MEGARENSIS PHILOSOPHI ACU-
TISSIMI MATHEMATICORUMQ̃ OMNIUM
SINE CONTROVERSIA PRINCIPIS OPA A
CAMPANO INTERPRETE FIDISSIMO TRA-
LATA, (*etc.*)

Venice: Paganinus, 11 June 1509.
Folio ($11\frac{1}{2} \times 8$ inches). Only edition.
Collation: a¹⁰; b-s⁸. Total: 146 leaves, last a blank.

In Latin, printed in roman type. One of the scarcest of all editions of Euclid which I have not had an opportunity of examining. The brief descriptions in the Libri Sale Catalogue (London, Sotheby, 1861), #2522 and 5477, and in Thomas-Stanford's *Early Editions of Euclid's Elements*, pp. 22-3, are the most complete I have been able to find. The work is illustrated with numerous large geometrical diagrams in the margins similar to those used in the *Summa de Arithmetica* editions of 1494 and 1523 by the same publisher. Thomas-Stanford says it is a very "attractive" book, with "ornamented capitals." The title—very like that of the *Divina Proportione*—is printed in red and black. Copies are at the Bodleian Library and the British Museum.

4

LA SCUOLA PERFETTA DEI MERCANTI

Venice: (printer?) 1504 or 1514.
Size: small 4to (?). Only edition.
Collation: not known except 246 leaves (?).

In Italian, type face unknown. As reported by Riccardi in the 1893 reprint of his *Biblioteca Matematica Italiana*, p. 115, Bonnani in his *Metodo facile di tenere i libri*, etc., Padua 1834, states that a certain Signor Andrea Vagner possessed, at that time, a copy of this "small work"—a rather badly printed volume of 246 leaves—printed at Venice in the year 1514. The text would seem to be a reprint of the chapter on book-keeping in the *Sūma de Arithmetica* of 1494. J. B. Geijsbeek (*Ancient Double Entry Book-keeping*, Denver, Colorado, 1914), pp. 5 and 8, while not having seen a copy himself, reports this book as printed at "Toscana" in 1504. Weight is given to this earlier date (the authority for which is not given) by the fact that the copyright of the *Sūma* expired in 1504 (ten years after it was granted) and not in 1514. The book is unfortunately apparently unknown to Brunet, Essling, and Dr Smith.

A SHORT LIST OF THE PRINCIPAL
REFERENCE WORKS

Atti dell' Accademia de' Nuovi Lincei, 1863.

Barciulli, F. Memorie...Luca Paciolo.

Bonnani. Metodo Facile di Tenere i Libri. Padua, 1834.

Brunet, J.-C. Manuel du Libraire. Paris, 1860, vol. i, p. 1116.

Corniani. I Secoli, vol. iii, p. 217.

Crivelli, P. English Translation of the Treatise on Double Entry Book-keeping by Frater Lucas Pacioli. London, 1924. Preface.

Essling, Prince d'. Les Livres à Figures Vénitiens. Florence and Paris, 1907 *et seq.*, vol. iii, pp. 185-7.

Geijsbeek, J. B. Ancient Double Entry Book-keeping. Denver, Colorado, 1914, pp. 5 and 8.

Hanan, E. Weigel. Archiv für die zeichn. Künste. 1856, vol. ii, pp. 231-44.

Jaeger, E. L. Der Traktat des L. Paccioli von 1494 über den Wechsel. Stuttgart, 1878.

Libri, G. Histoire des Sciences Mathématiques. Paris, 1835-41, vol. iii, pp. 277-94.

—— Sotheby's Sale Catalogue. London, 1861, #578, #2522, and #5475-7 inclusive.

Manzoni, G. Studii di Bibliografia Analitica.

de Morgan, A. Arithmetical Books. London, 1847, p. 2.

Morison, S. Article in Encyclopaedia Britannica, 14th ed., vol. iv, p. 615, and bibliography, pp. 617-18.

Morley's Life of Cardan, vol. i, pp. 213-14.

Narducci. Intorno a due Edizioni della Summa de Arithmetica di Fra Luca Pacioli, etc. Rome, 1862.

Pollard, A. W. Italian...Early Printing: A Catalogue of... the Library of C. W. Dyson-Perrins. Oxford, 1914, pp. 160-1.

Riccardi, P.   Biblioteca Matematica Italiana. Modena, 1870, vol. ii, Part i, pp. 226-30 incl. And 1893 edition, p. 115.

Smith, David Eugene.   Rara Arithmetica, pp. 54-9 incl., and pp. 87 and 89.

Thomas-Stanford, Charles.   Early Editions of Euclid's Elements. The Bibliographical Society, London, 1926, pp. 6, 22-3, and plates 5 and 6.

Tiraboschi, V.   Storia, vol. vi, p. 554.

Vermiglioli.   Biografia, vol. i, p. 214.

Vianello, V.   Luca Paccioli nella storia della ragioneria, etc. Messina, 1896.

Winship, Geo. P.   Census of Fifteenth Century Books Owned in America. New York, 1919.

Winterburg, C.   Fra Luca Pacioli. In Quellenschriften für Kunstgeschichte, etc. Vienna, 1889.

Also see the standard reference works; Hain (#4105), Pellechet (#3060), Proctor (#5168), etc., for the incunable edition of the Sūma de Arithmetica, 1494.

INDEX

❧ INDEX ❧

Ye Olde Tea Shoppe

8 th

1st

of

Phil Toft

· 1999 ·